SOCK MONKEY
BOOGIE-WOOGIE

Cece Bell

CANDLEWICK PRESS

For Granny Bell, Mary Ann,
and Sarah

Copyright © 2004 by Cece Bell

First edition in this format 2015

Library of Congress Cataloging-in-Publication Data is available.
Library of Congress Catalog Card Number 2003069564

ISBN 978-0-7636-2392-0 (original hardcover)
ISBN 978-0-7636-7758-9 (reformatted hardcover)

15 16 17 18 19 20 CCP 10 9 8 7 6 5 4 3 2 1

Printed in Shenzhen, Guangdong, China

This book was typeset in Cafeteria.
The illustrations were created digitally.

Candlewick Press
99 Dover Street
Somerville, Massachusetts 02144

visit us at www.candlewick.com

Sock Monkey, the famous toy actor, was going to the Big Celebrity Dance, and he just couldn't wait.

But there was one problem. He needed a dance partner.

He'd ask Blue Pig, but he was going on a business trip.

He'd ask Froggie, but he was visiting family.

And he'd ask Miss Bunn, but she was taking a vacation.

All his friends were leaving!

Don't worry—you'll find a dance partner!

The next day, Sock Monkey was lonesome . . .

and he still didn't know what to do about the big dance.

So Sock Monkey decided to find a dance partner on his own. He put up a big sign, and he waited.

He didn't have to wait long.

WANTED:
GOOD DANCER to dance with Sock Monkey (famous actor) at the BIG CELEBRITY DANCE!

Just about every toy in town responded to Sock Monkey's sign.

Too tall!

Too small!

Too dizzy!

Too busy!

Unfortunately, the auditions did not go so well.

Too clunky!

Too funky!

Bad breath.

Oh no! I'm doomed! I'll never find a dance partner — never!

What was Sock Monkey going to do?
Just when he felt nothing could go right,
three packages arrived.

They were gifts from his friends!

Miss Bunn gave him a beautiful hat and sweater,
Blue Pig mailed a pair of enormous socks, and
Froggie sent cotton from his family's farm.

As Sock Monkey admired his gifts, a wonderful idea began to form in his head.

AHA!

He knew exactly what to do!

The first thing Sock Monkey did was cut the buttons off his new sweater . . .

and he unraveled it until he had a big ball of yarn.

Next he turned the socks inside out. Then he cut . . .

and he sewed them with the yarn . . .

and he stuffed everything with cotton …

until at last, he had finished his masterpiece.

Sock Monkey had made another monkey . . .

and maybe the perfect dance partner!

Sock Monkey couldn't believe his luck — Sock Buddy was
a fast learner. He could really shimmy!

When Sock Monkey and Sock Buddy were finally on their way to the Big Celebrity Dance, they could hardly hide their excitement.

They pulled up to the dance club in Sock Monkey's fancy new convertible.

The doorman was impressed.

Inside, Sock Monkey was interviewed for TV, and he proudly presented his dance partner to the whole world.

Sock Buddy had never seen so many toys before.
He wanted to run to the nearest exit.

At first, Sock Monkey and Sock Buddy had a little trouble warming up.

But soon, they remembered all the boogie-woogie moves they'd practiced.

The dance was amazing — and over all too soon.
On the way home, Sock Monkey told Sock Buddy that
tomorrow was another big day. Miss Bunn, Blue Pig, and
Froggie would be coming home!

And when — at last — his friends returned, Sock Monkey was thrilled to see them again.

When Sock Monkey introduced Miss Bunn, Froggie, and Blue Pig to Sock Buddy, they liked him right away.

They felt as if they had known him forever.

THE END